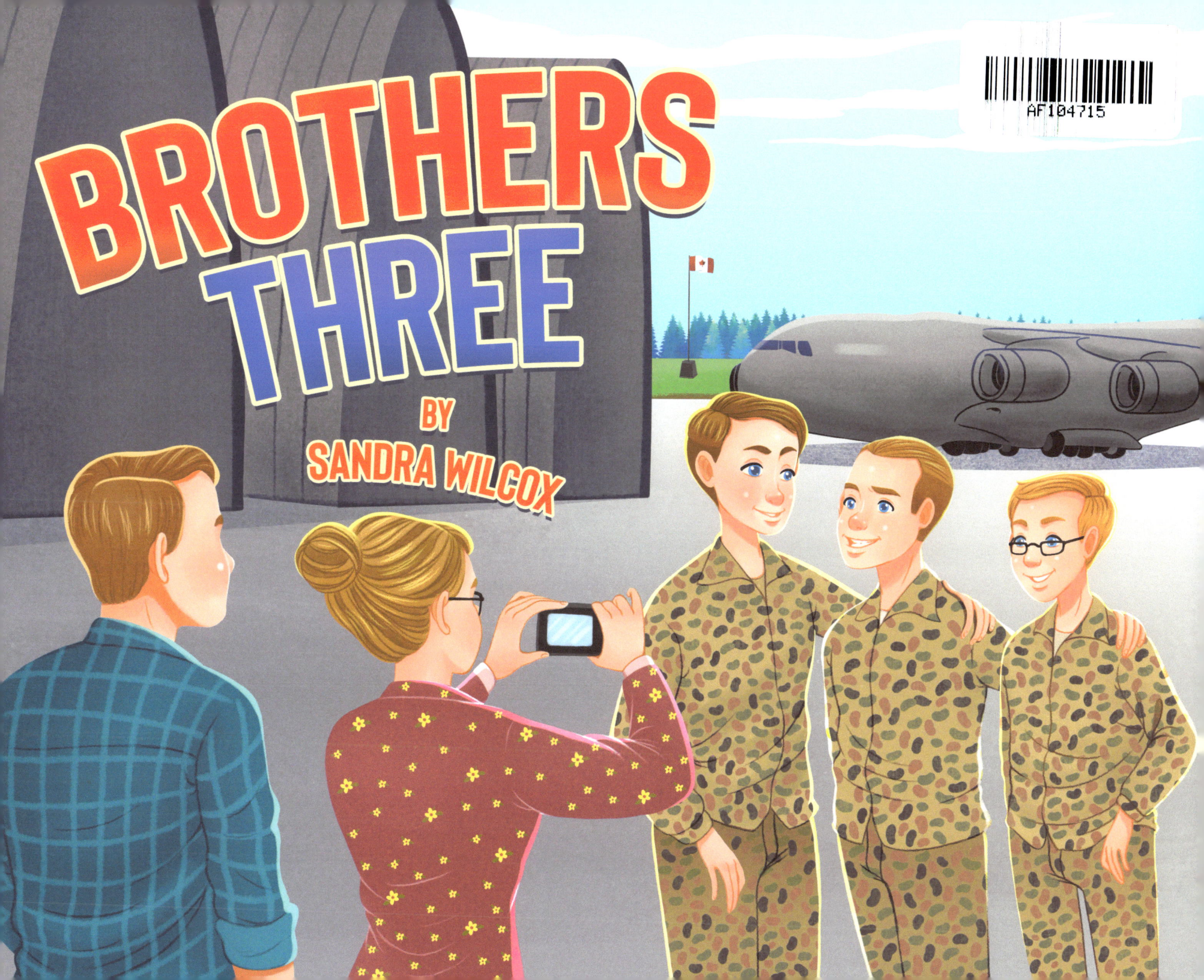

Brothers Three
Copyright © 2019 by Sandra Wilcox

All rights reserved. No part of this publication may be reproduced, distributed, or transmitted in any form or by any means, including photocopying, recording, or other electronic or mechanical methods, without the prior written permission of the author, except in the case of brief quotations embodied in critical reviews and certain other non-commercial uses permitted by copyright law.

Tellwell Talent
www.tellwell.ca

ISBN
978-0-2288-1561-7 (Paperback)

Grandchild come, sit upon my knee
I'll tell you the tale of the brothers three.
Born to a couple, who felt blessed with each boy,
A good father's pride, and a proud mother's joy.

The eldest son with hair like gold,
was kissed by angels, so the legend goes.
He was blessed with the looks of a great golden statue.
and your knees turned to liquid, when he cast his gaze at you.

The second in line, had eyes of soft brown,
and his heart, it is said, was as soft as goose down.
A radiance shone from within him, they say,
which could rival the sun on a hot summer day.

The youngest was born on a dark stormy night.
He had a thirst for all knowledge, and the gift of foresight.
His hunger for humour could never be sated,
and a man so well loved, could never be hated.
The three boys grew up
with so much love in their hearts
When asked to serve their country,
They couldn't wait to depart.

Off to the battle,
the three brothers fled.
They fought with the blessings
Of the heavens, it's said.

For years, the brothers fought
And gave it their all.
They fought with conviction
As they watched their friends fall.

When the war finally ended
and the brothers returned.
The eldest mans beauty
Was melted and burned

His angelic face,
once framed with gold hair
was scarred, red, and blackened,
and caused people to stare.

The second of sons
had been blinded and maimed.
The visions of horror
could never be tamed.

His inner light dimmed
and his soft heart grew cold
as the horrors he'd witnessed
might someday be told.

The third of the three,
who was blessed with foresight,
was driven mad with the knowledge,
there's no escaping the fight.

The laughter was silenced
with the sound of the dead,
which grew constantly louder
with each rising from bed.

But the changes we see
in the brothers three,
were sacrificed gladly
so we could be free.

Grandchild mine,
asleep on my knee
you're safe in your dreams
with the brothers three.

www.ingramcontent.com/pod-product-compliance
Lightning Source LLC
LaVergne TN
LVHW071733060526
838200LV00031B/488